DIFFERENT FOR BOYS

DIFFERENT FOR BOYS

PATRICK NESS

illustrated by

TEA BENDIX

WALKER BOOKS

Text copyright © 2010, 2023 by Patrick Ness
Illustrations copyright © 2020 by Tea Bendix

First US edition 2023
First published in *Losing It*, edited by Keith Gray (London: Andersen Press, 2010), and in updated form in Danish as *Anderledes med drenge* (Hamburg, Germany: Carlsen, 2020)

Library of Congress Catalog Card Number 2022915226
ISBN 978-1-5362-2889-2

22 23 24 25 26 27 APS 10 9 8 7 6 5 4 3 2 1

Printed in Humen, Dongguan, China

This book was typeset in Adobe Jenson Pro.
The illustrations were done in pencil and digital collage.

Walker Books US
a division of
Candlewick Press
99 Dover Street
Somerville, Massachusetts 02144

www.walkerbooksus.com

For Nick

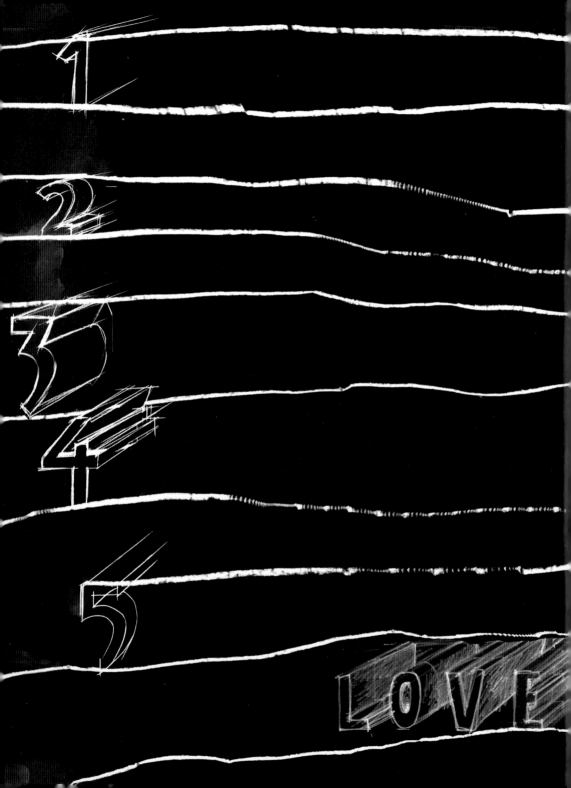

THE LIST

All right then, if we're starting out honest, here's pretty much everything I've done (it's not as bad as it sounds):

1. I've ████████████, of course. Everyone ████████████. They're lying if they say they don't, but ████████████ doesn't count, obviously. You can't lose your virginity to yourself.

2. And leading on from that, I've been ████████ by someone else, but who's been to a freshman year party and not gone home without doing *that* in the coat pile? It's only someone's hands.

3. Getting a bit heavier, I've ████ and ████. Still not really a shocker.

4. A bit more strangely, I've ████████████ ████████████████████████████ ████████████████████████████ ████████████████████. (Okay, I'm not

allowed to even hint at the strange stuff. Not that kind of story. Fine.)

5. And of course we wouldn't be talking about this if I hadn't actually ███. You know, actually ████████████████████████,

which is pretty much the definition of losing your virginity if you're a boy.

And just so we're clear, it's not like I've done #5 once or twice either. I'm not one of those chess club virgins who goes into a closet and wonders if the real thing's happened. It has. Trust me. Although it doesn't really matter how many times you do it: you think it's going to make your life less lonely, but it never does.

I suppose my question, though, is where exactly on that list did I stop being a virgin?

Is it obviously #5? Or can it happen sooner, like on #3? Or even #2?

Are there degrees of virginity? Is there a points system? A league table?

And who gets to say?

Because maybe it's not as clear as all that, maybe there's more to it. Maybe there are people who'd *still* say I'm a virgin, even after doing numbers 1 through 5.

In fact, I might be one of those people.

WHERE IT STARTS

There are lots of places this story could start, but it might as well start on the first day of junior year, when Charlie and me are sitting in AP history, waiting for Mr. Bacon to get his seating plan finished.

"Well, this is taking ███████ forever," Charlie says, then he blinks, surprised. "What the ███████ just happened? What are these ███████ black boxes?"

I shrug. "It's that kind of story. Certain words are necessary because this is real life, but you can't actually *show* 'em because we're too young to read about the stuff we actually do, right?"

"Teens swear in stories these days."

"Not anything like we do in reality," I say. "It's the difference between shooting a bullet and throwing it."

Charlie nods solemnly at the truth of this. Then he gets a smirk.

"████████████████████████," he says. His

smile gets bigger. "████████████████████████ ████ ██████████." He nods again. "Cool."

And just as he says, "Cool," that's when Josh Smith walks in, which is where this all *really* starts.

"No ████████ *way*," Charlie says.

We watch Josh check in with Mr. Bacon, who finds his name on the list and points him toward me and Charlie. Mr. Bacon's great new idea for this year has us sitting in "quads" rather than just boring rows. Four desks pushed together in little islands around the room. Says it's supposed to make learning "collaborative," but any fool could see he won't be able to control us like this.

The quads are alphabetical, so I – being Ant Stevenson – am sitting with Charlie Shepton, who I've sat by alphabetically since elementary school. And now here's Josh Smith, who Charlie and I were also alphabetical friends with from way back, too, before he left after fifth grade to move to Spokane with his dad.

"Charlie Shepton and Ant Stevenson," Josh Smith says, coming over to us, grinning.

"Josh ███████ Smith!" Charlie says, standing up and punching Josh on the shoulder, even though Josh is now twice his size. Josh, in fact, is even bigger than me, not in any fat way, but like he just stepped off the Super Bowl plane to buy a pack of cigarettes. "Where the ████ have you been keeping yourself?" Charlie asks. "It's been ███████ ages."

"Watch your language, Charlie," says Mr. Bacon from the front. "That's your first warning. Now, sit."

"But it's blacked out, sir," Charlie says. "It's like I'm not swearing at all. ████. See?"

"*Sit*," Mr. Bacon says.

"Mom and Dad got back together," Josh explains as we all sit down. "After seven years, if you can believe it." His eyes stray across the crowded classroom. "Hey, don't tell me the fourth is going to be little Jack Taylor."

"Aw, ████," Charlie says, as we see Jack Taylor already being directed over to our quad by Mr. Bacon.

"What?" Josh says to me, confused. "It'll be just like old times."

Because the thing you need to know is that the four of us, me and Charlie and Josh Smith and Jack Taylor, used to be inseparable. All through elementary, anyway. Besides always sitting next to each other because of our names, we lived on the same few streets, and for a while there, we were always together. Birthday parties and Little League teams and just plain old stupid hanging around.

Then Josh left and a few years later puberty hit and I suddenly got way bigger than everybody, like linebacker big, and Charlie got a foot taller without gaining any weight, and Jack, well, Jack didn't grow all that much, and though me and Charlie stayed friends, Jack kinda went his own way when we all went on to high school. And while Charlie and me just did the usual – soccer, skipping class, more soccer – Jack, well . . .

Jack got a little . . . *dramatic*, if I'm honest.

He joined drama club. And choir. And wrote opera reviews for the school newspaper. And he always picked Mark Ruffalo as best out of the Avengers, when, I mean, come on. Hemsworth is standing right there.

I don't mean any of that in a bad way, though.

Because you don't really notice when it happens over time, do you? Jack's your friend. You like him because you've always liked him. And maybe one day you think, yeah, okay, he's gone a bit pink, but so what? He's Jack. And most of the time, you don't even notice.

Unless you're Charlie, and one day, you start noticing. Even in this day and age. When we're all supposed to be beyond all that.

From about last Christmas, Charlie's started noticing. And he isn't handling it well.

"Jack's a little ███████ homo now," he says as we watch Jack come over. "Hey, you can say *homo* without the box. That doesn't seem right."

Josh raises his eyebrows. "Jack turned out gay?"

"No," I say. "He went out with Georgina Harcourt all last year. He's just kinda flamboyant."

"He's ████████ *gay*," Charlie says. "He was caught ███ ███████ to a bunch of seniors last year."

"No, he *wasn't*," I say. "Claudia Templeton spread that

story to stop people from talking about how her boyfriend texted around all those pictures of her ████."

"Oh, yeah." Charlie laughs. "That was *cool*."

"If it isn't Josh Smith," Jack says, dropping his bag on the fourth desk in our quad.

"Hey, Jack," Josh says. "Heard you've gone all Neil Patrick Harris on us."

Jack shoots a glare at Charlie. "I see you've been talking to ████ here."

"Hey!" Charlie says. "What was behind the box?"

"Hey, Jack," I say, nodding a greeting.

"Hey, Ant." He nods back, a little carefully.

"Neil Patrick Harris is a rich man, Jack," Josh says, still smiling. "Nothing to be ashamed of."

"Please," Jack says. "He's shaped like a scarecrow. Plus, his face makes me angry." He gives Josh a look up and down. "And where've *you* been? Eating your way through eastern Washington?"

"Aw, hell, don't even start," Josh says. "I wasn't on school grounds five minutes this morning before the football coach grabbed me." He nods my way. "You've gotten pretty big yourself, Ant. You should try out for the team with me. Be nice to have an old friend around."

"We play soccer," Charlie says, before I can even answer.

"Quiet in the back," Mr. Bacon calls over to us, finally ready to start class.

"So who's this guy?" Josh says, lowering his voice.

I shrug. "Just Mr. Bacon."

Josh frowns. "He looks familiar."

"Nah," Jack says. "He just looks like if Eddie Redmayne was a serial killer."

"God, Jack," Josh says. "That's it exactly."

Despite ourselves, we all see it. You could totally picture your sister dating Mr. Bacon, but then you could totally see him strangling her, too. I'm about to say so, but then Charlie sneers, "You want to *date* him, Jack? You want him to ████ you right there on his desk?"

Jack looks fake surprised. "Are you *flirting* with me, Shepton?"

Josh snorts under his breath. I laugh a little, too.

And then I see Charlie giving me a look that could poison a whole tank of fish.

CHARLIE

Charlie isn't a bad guy. He isn't, despite how he's acting and what's going to happen in the rest of this story. He's just got . . . *issues*. I mean, I know, yeah, fine, everybody's got issues, but Charlie's issues aren't too nice to him and they give him a rough time and that sometimes makes him act like a total ██.

But he's not a bad guy. He isn't. If the world were better, Charlie would be better. Try to remember that when the ██ starts hitting the fan, okay?

Plus he's my friend. I've known him for a long, long time, and that counts for something.

"How cool is it that Josh is back?" I say, sitting on my bed. We've come over to my house and gone up to my room, firing up my dad's old laptop that I got instead of the MacBook I asked for. We can see it over there, failing to find the wireless signal floating around the house.

"Yeah," Charlie says, nodding. He's sprawled on my

floor, bouncing a soccer ball up and down. "The █████ size of him, though. Did you see?"

"Not much bigger than me," I say.

"Bigger," Charlie says. "But you're fatter."

"Screw you," I say. "I'm not fat."

I'm not. Really, I'm not. I'm just big. I'm not fat.

"Jack Taylor's a █████, though, isn't he?" Charlie says, frowning.

"What do you mean?"

"The way he was practically *hanging* on Josh. It was █████ embarrassing."

"Ah, Jack's all right," I say. "Leave him alone."

"It shouldn't be allowed," Charlie says. "A homo like that. *Sashaying* around school like Troye █████ Sivan."

"A lot of people like Troye Sivan. Nobody cares about that stuff anymore."

"In Seattle, maybe, or Los Angeles. Not out here in the ass end of nowhere."

"Wouldn't that be exactly where gay people hang out, though?" I say (please don't judge me, not yet anyway). "The ass end?"

And we laugh at that for a while because we're young and stupid and we like laughing at stupid ██████.

"That was classic," Charlie says, still laughing.

The laptop makes a sudden pinging sound and the screen goes black. "Not *again*," I moan, sitting up.

"Leave it," Charlie says, resignation in his voice.

And then he's silent in a way where somehow I know what it means.

You ever noticed that about silence? That sometimes you can just tell what kind of silence it is? Sometimes silence is real loud, louder than anything.

Charlie's silence, for example, right now, right here, is asking me something, even though he hasn't said a thing.

And so I answer him.

"Yeah," I say. "Okay."

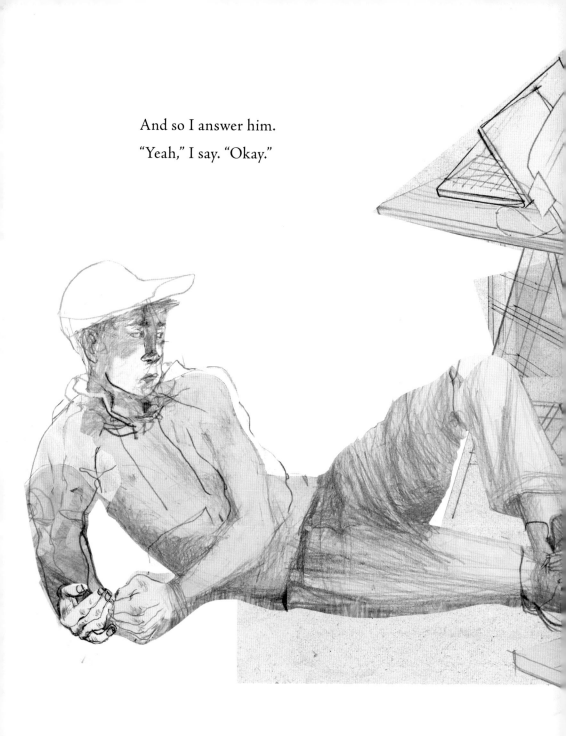

THE LIST AGAIN

You remember that list of all the things I've done? How long it was?

Everything on it, I've done with Charlie.

LAST CHRISTMAS

It started last Christmas. Charlie called and asked if he could come over because his mom was getting even more drunk than usual. His dad's long gone, see, and his mom drinks. Nothing too special or interesting, but it doesn't mean it's not hard for Charlie just because it's common.

Anyway, my mom and dad know Charlie's mom, so they said yes pretty easily and he came over with every present he got, including a Switch, because he was afraid his mom'd get into her firebug frame of mind again, which she did once with all his school clothes in eighth grade (really; he had to borrow some of mine for *weeks*, made him look like a skeleton).

He ended up staying most of the week before New Year's. Do you know how many times Charlie's mom called to check on him? Don't ask.

He slept on the floor of my room and we'd stay up all night talking and playing on the Switch and going online.

You know, the usual stuff.

And then one night Charlie was on a porn site. Nothing weird, just your run-of-the-mill naked girls. We'd done it before, plenty of times, but this time Charlie started talking. Talking about sex and girls and how long it'd been since he'd ███████████████████████████████████
██████████████████████████████████████
██████████████████████████████████████
██████████████████████████████████████
██████████████████████████████████████
██████████████████████████████████████
████████████████████.

Oh. I guess I can't tell you how we led up to it (in case anyone uses it as a road map, horror of horrors, as if there aren't nine thousand and one examples of boys and *girls* our age getting together on every possible level; you can find that on Disney+, for Christ's sake).

Whatever. Just to say that we were laughing about it all, like it was all a big joke.

And then there was this moment where it wasn't a joke,

not even remotely, and it could have gone any way, in any direction, and let's just say, I was surprised at the one it took. Not necessarily because I didn't want to, but because it was *Charlie*.

Immediately after, it was like he didn't want to look me in the eye, though, and the next morning, he went right back to his house, taking all his stuff. We didn't talk at all until we were back in school and the first days were awkward and quiet and it took a while before things were back to normal.

Then it was spring break. Charlie asked if he could come over again. That time, it was easier to look each other in the eye. And that's how it's pretty much gone since Christmas.

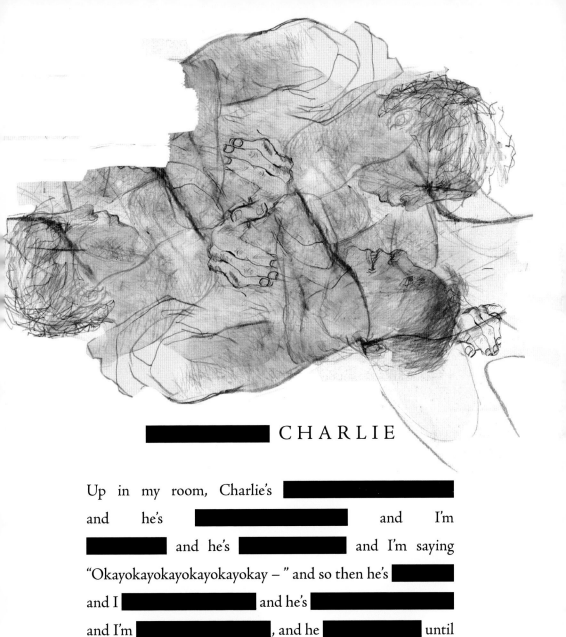

████████████ CHARLIE

Up in my room, Charlie's ██████████████████
and he's ████████████████ and I'm
████████ and he's ██████████ and I'm saying
"Okayokayokayokayokayokay – " and so then he's ████████
and I ████████████ and he's ████████████████
and I'm ██████████████ , and he ██████████ until
he finally ████████████████ , too.

And then we're both breathing heavy and sweating from it all and he looks up at me and he gets this grin, this shy, embarrassed grin that makes you forgive Charlie everything but that also says, "Well, *that* was fun," and says everything about how ridiculous it is for us both to be here like this, doing what we've just done. Every time, Charlie makes it clear we're just goofing around, that it's just a release until we both get girlfriends, and we spend most of our time trying to pretend we aren't taking it seriously at all.

Except for those few minutes when it's the most serious thing on earth.

"Soccer starts next week," Charlie says after a while.

"Yeah," I say.

"We better ████████ make varsity."

"Yeah, right," I say.

"No, I'm ████████ serious," he says. "I'm sick to ████ death of JV. And we're both about a foot ████████ taller than last year. That ought to count for something."

"You might make
striker," I say. "There's no
way I'm making goalie over
Olly Barton."

He looks over at me. "Have you seen yourself lately? You tower over Olly Barton now."

"He's faster."

"You're bigger. You'll beat him into the ██████ ground. Then we'll finally be on a decent team together."

"If I'm so big," I say, "maybe I should join Josh on football this year."

He looks surprised for a second, but then he sees I'm not serious. "You'd get your fat ██ kicked," he says, laughing. He looks up at my ceiling. "Nah, you'll see," he says. "The two of us on varsity together. Un-██████-stoppable." Then he turns to me with his shy, embarrassed grin again.

And that's the Charlie no one knows but me. The one who grins like that. And I want to kiss that grin so bad I could cry.

But that's the one thing we don't do. Despite all that we've done, everything on that list, he won't kiss me. He refuses, so harshly I've only asked twice and not since Christmas.

We can't kiss.

Because that would make us gay.

Gay like Charlie sees all over Jack Taylor.

MARK RUFFALO

"Mark Ruffalo?" Josh says.

"He's the best actor in the Avengers," Jack says. "Plus he fights for the environment and stuff. He's an admirable guy."

"So's Obama," Josh says, "but you don't see me carrying around pictures of him."

"I'm not *carrying around* a picture of him," Jack says. "It's for a project."

"A project on the Avengers?"

Jack sighs. "It's for Drama. We had to pick someone real to impersonate."

"So let's hear it."

"Hi, I'm Mark Ruffalo."

Josh laughs, but not in a mean way. "Shoulda picked Hemsworth. Australian's easy."

"Easier than what?" Charlie says, sitting down in the quad with us.

"Than sounding like this dude," Josh says, nabbing the magazine cutout he'd spotted in Jack's papers and holding it up.

"That's just Jack's boyfriend," Charlie says. "He's got a thing for old men."

"Mark's not old," Jack says, a bit too fast. "He's fifty-four."

There's an awkward pause at how Jack knows this. And for how he called him Mark, too.

"You're ██████ sick," Charlie says. "He's old enough to be your dad."

"My father is seventy-one," Jack says.

Josh looks surprised. "Really?"

"Mom was his third wife," Jack says. "She 'forgot' to take the pill one year. Now he's with wife number four. Which is weird, because wife number four looks like a linebacker."

Josh snaps his fingers like he's remembered something. "Ant! I meant to tell you, I talked to the football coach, and he's all for you trying out."

Charlie looks up sharply at this.

"I'm serious," Josh says. "You could easily make second string, maybe even start."

"Me and Ant play soccer," Charlie cuts in. "Always have."

Josh shrugs. "Doesn't mean you always have to. Ant's grown into the right shape. Might be time for a change."

Charlie looks at me. "But we've always played soccer."

"I wouldn't be any good at football," I say to Josh. "I don't run very fast."

"And that makes you good at soccer?" Josh asks. "Come with me next week, give it a try. You might like it."

"We've got *soccer* starting up," Charlie says, as if Josh isn't understanding the point.

"You should join the debate team, Charlie," Jack says. "Your subtlety of thought is all they're missing to take them to the top."

"Enough chatter, boys," Mr. Bacon says, suddenly appearing at our quad. "Or I'll put you all in detention. You too, Jack."

"Aw, Mr. Bacon," Jack says, all smiles. "And besmirch my perfect record? You'd do that to a handsome boy like me?"

"Even a boy like you," Mr. Bacon says, smiling back despite himself.

We're all quiet as Jack watches Mr. Bacon walk away for just a second too long.

"You little ██████ *sicko*," Charlie says under his breath.

"What?" Jack says. "I'm going to copy his walk for when I do Mark Ruffalo."

Josh and I laugh, but Charlie just says, "██████ freak."

Jack stares at him for a long, hard second, then he says, talking to me but looking at Charlie, "I think you should definitely try out for football, Ant."

WALKING HOME

"I swear to God," Charlie says as we walk home that day, "someone needs to kick that little ████'s ass."

"Jack's pretty tough, though," I say, trying to make a joke of it. "You sure you could take him?"

Which is the wrong thing to say, of course. "Just because I'm not some ██████ mutant giant like you and your new best friend Josh?" Charlie says.

"He's not my new best friend," I say. "Anyway, he's your friend, too."

"He's probably a ██████ homo just like Jack ███████ Taylor. They're probably going off to ████ each other right now."

"What?" I say, getting annoyed. "You mean like *we* are?"

He stops right there on the pavement and glares at me. "████ you," he says. "I'm not a ██████ homo."

"Then why do you keep talking about Jack Taylor?" I say.

He keeps glaring at me, but then he says something I don't expect him to say. "You trying out for football?"

I blink. "What?" I say. "No."

"You trying out for *football*?" he asks again, even more angry.

I pause, a second too long, maybe because, yeah, okay, I had thought it might be fun playing football for a change, because Josh asked the coach about me, and Josh, well, never mind about Josh.

But I can see what Charlie's asking me.

"No way," I say. "You and me on varsity this year. Un-███████-stoppable."

"Too ██████ right," Charlie says.

And one more time, there's that grin. He looks like he regrets it, but he grins anyway.

The grin that makes my heart hurt a little bit.

More than a little.

QUESTIONS

And so do you see what I mean about the list? If Charlie and I are just doing all this as fill-in until the "real thing" comes along, what does that mean? Does it mean what me and Charlie do isn't real somehow? That we aren't really doing it to each other, but to some imaginary future girl? That no matter how much you go to soccer practice, it isn't really soccer until it's an actual match?

Have I even lost my virginity? Or am I just a virgin with a lot of practice? Because that's the way it sometimes feels.

And does wanting to kiss Charlie mean anything if he doesn't want to kiss me back?

ONE MORE QUESTION

And by the way, is it spelled *homos* like *promos?* Or *homoes* like *heroes?*

Who would know?

WHAT KIND OF STORY
THIS IS

One more thing before we get back to what happens. You know what Charlie said back there about Josh and Jack? How they're both probably homos? (Homoes? Seriously, is there someone I can ask?)

Well, okay, this is the kind of story where we can tell the truth, even if it is behind black boxes, so that's a good thing, but it does mean there's a whole bunch of things that this story definitely *isn't*, okay?

For example, this isn't one of those stories where one of us hunky young dudes has lots of life-changing sex with Mr. Bacon. First of all, *yuck*. Second of all, that only happens in stories written by horny middle-aged writers who think they look like Mr. Bacon, all right? Doesn't happen in real life, and it's so not going to happen here. And third, seriously, *yuck*.

This also isn't going to be one of those stories where the great big tough football guy turns out to be a really self-confident homo who happily gets off with your humble narrator, much as that might be nice for certain humble narrators. I mean, yeah, the big football guys are gay just as often as everybody else, but I guess most of them wait until college to figure it out. Then they all move to Seattle and join gyms.

And finally, this isn't going to be one of those stories where everyone learns a lesson because the little drama fella turns out to be a total ladies' man. Jack did go out with Georgina Harcourt for all of last year, and I think they may have actually done the deed. I also know more than one girl who wants to go out with him, too, and they all say, "Nuh-uh, no way he's gay, he's just mature and sooo sensitive," and then their eyes go all misty as they picture him as the perfect husband who'll listen to their problems and watch all the same rom-coms.

And that's probably true, some of the time. But not here.

In real life, sometimes the big straight guy is just a big straight guy, and sometimes the kid that seems gay *is* gay.

Doesn't mean they're not still nice people.

Jack is gay.

I know, because last summer, he told me.

And in return, I lied to him.

SEX TALK

"I'm telling you," Charlie's saying. "Five times. Five times in one hour."

"Bull████," Jack says. "You can't even ████ five times in an hour."

"Oh, Jack," Josh says next to him, shaking his head sadly. "There's so many things wrong with that sentence, I don't even know where to begin."

You know, the way teenage guys talk about sex, you'd think all of us were having it all the time, nonstop. Okay, some of us probably *are*, but not nearly as many as brag about it. Maybe there's a boy who's enough of a moron to take a picture of his ████ and send it to his girlfriend and that picture gets passed around to *everyone*, and sure, there's the internet where sex is everywhere, but maybe people aren't actually having it any more than they used to. Maybe they just have better material to lie with.

For instance, Charlie's never had a girl, not as far as I know, not all the way, but he can talk about it like a porno director.

"Five times in an hour is nothing," Charlie says. "Not if the girl is a total hot ███."

"Says the voice of experience," Jack says. "You've never had sex with anything besides your own hand, Shepton."

"I think you're thinking of yourself there, Jack," Josh says, then he makes a ███ motion with his hand. "'Oh, Mark Ruffalo. Come and do me but, you know, as the Hulk.'"

Even Jack laughs at this, but then Charlie says, "Jack's too busy ███ half the teachers' lounge to need to ███."

"The other half," Jack says, "being otherwise occupied passing your bony ██ around."

Charlie's face gets red. "You little ███. You little ███ homo."

"Oh Jesus, Shepton," Jack says, rolling his eyes. "Why don't you just ask me out and be done with it?"

And me and Josh are still laughing. But Charlie's not laughing at all.

He leans forward across the desks, getting his face up into Jack's. "You're ███████ gay," Charlie says. "Everyone ███████ knows it. You can sit here and you can pretend to joke with the rest of us but you're a ███████ homo and there's going to come a day when someone takes you down."

But Jack doesn't back off. He just leans forward, too, and without taking his eyes off Charlie, blows him a kiss.

Which turns out to be a step too far.

Because suddenly Jack is falling back as Charlie lunges for him over the desks and Josh is already on his feet, way faster than you'd think for such a big guy – no wonder the football coach wants him – and he's already between Charlie and Jack, holding Charlie back.

"I'm going to ███████ stomp you into the ███████ ground, you little ████████!"

Charlie's yelling and Josh is still holding him back and Mr. Bacon's charging over and pulling them apart, too, and as Mr. Bacon and Josh start dragging Charlie to the door to send him to the vice principal, Jack looks up at me from where he's sitting on the floor.

"Oops," he says.

JACK

It was one Saturday afternoon this past summer. I was supposed to go to the movies with Charlie but then his mom did something he wouldn't explain and suddenly I'm at the theater by myself, yelling at Charlie over my cell for not showing up and thinking I should just go home because what kind of loser sees a movie by himself? But then who shows up but Jack.

By himself.

"Where's Georgina?" I asked him.

"We broke up," he said. "It's cool, though. We're friends."

"Uh-huh," I said.

And it was weird, you know, because like I said, I've known Jack since we were kids, since we used to call him Jackie, and though we'd grown apart as we got older, it was never like we'd had a falling out, and though he was already the gayest-seeming kid in the whole school, it's not like I was ashamed of him or anything.

Well, maybe a little, maybe for reasons that are completely obvious.

But that little bit of embarrassment only made me feel bad. Plus, there was no one else around from our school, so Jack and I went to the movie together, some incredibly stupid piece of ███ about romantic vampires, five minutes into which Jack started making jokes and we pretty much laughed all the way through, getting shushed by the nine billion girls sitting around us.

And after, of course, we were on the same bus back home and it seemed the natural thing to do to invite Jack in. Mom was delighted to see him – Jack was always the most polite of all my friends – and she made us sandwiches, which we took up to my room. I fired up the wheezing laptop and we started gaming.

Which, apparently for me, is the cue for people to start Really Important Conversations.

"You know you can meet people on apps? Even in this little town?" Jack said after we'd spent way too long looking up facts about Mark Ruffalo. Did you know he's deaf in one ear?

Of course you didn't. Why would you? Why would *anyone*?

"People like who?" I said.

Jack shrugged. "People." And was silent.

"You mean like . . . Facebook?"

He gave me a look to tell me to stop being such an idiot because it was screamingly obvious that I was pretending to be stupid. "Yeah," he said, "Facebook – where everyone is over fifty and watches *The Bachelor*."

"Then what do you mean?" I said, laughing, because that's totally what Facebook is.

"I mean real people," he said. "You can *meet* real people."

"And do what?"

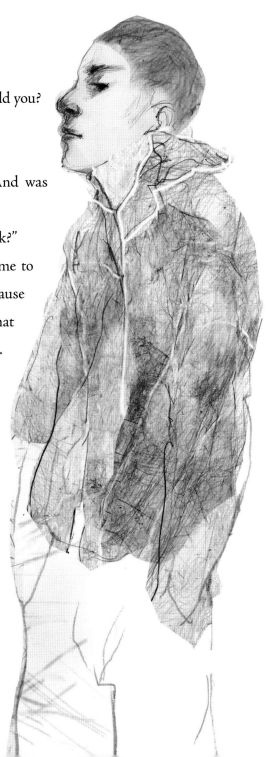

55

He gave me another idiot look.

And then I finally realized.

"Jack, you're not talking about . . ." I sat up. "You're not getting groomed, are you?"

He rolled his eyes. "*Groomed*. Please."

"What are you talking about, then?"

And still he didn't say anything.

"Jesus, Jack," I said. "What kind of sleazy ███ is going to meet up with a fifteen-year-old boy on an app? You're asking to get yourself killed."

"I haven't done anything," he said, backpedaling. "I haven't actually *met* anyone. You know. Women."

And it was that word, *women*, that made it all clear, because it was such a false word just then, like he was suddenly trying to pretend we weren't talking about what we were obviously talking about.

"You're lying," I said, my voice low. "You've met up with people." I reached out and grabbed his arm to make him look at me. "You've met up with men, haven't you?"

He jerked his arm away from me.

But he didn't deny it.

"Jack," I said. "That's so dangerous, dude. I'm not trying to be a teacher here, but you could get your throat slit. You could get *raped*, Jack. Please don't tell me – "

"Just once," he said, quiet enough to make me shut up. "I've only met someone once." He cleared his throat. "It was horrible. Worse than you even think."

"Jack – "

"And so I haven't done it again, all right?" he said, defensive now. "I mean, do you have any idea how unbelievably ████████ *lonely* it gets? Feeling like you're the only one? It's not like I've got a lot of options for meeting people my own age, now do I?"

And then he looked at me. In a way that made me lean back.

And there was a silence that, once again, I knew was asking me something.

Asking me loud and clear.

This is just this past summer, remember? Two months ago. The summer where I'd already been ████████ Charlie regularly since Christmas.

And here was one of my oldest friends, someone who I didn't have a thing against in the world, someone who was fun to be around and who'd never been anything but a good person to me.

And of course I ███████ knew how lonely it got.

(Jesus *Christ*, just that word, *lonely*, makes me feel so empty I don't even want to talk about it.)

I'd heard there were some gay girls in senior year who were dating each other right out in the open. But not any boys. It's different for boys. I mean, everybody knows somebody gay – duh, it's not 1980 or something – but not at school. At school, it was a secret, and you were on your own. I knew exactly how Jack felt. Of *course* I did.

Why do you think I was spending all that time with Charlie?

But I lied.

God damn me to my dying day, because the biggest sin you can commit is failing a friend. But that's what I did.

I failed him.

"Sorry," I said. "I'm not gay."

Jack held on to my gaze. "No? I thought maybe . . ."

I shook my head. "No, dude. Sorry."

He just nodded. "I'm sorry, too," he said.

I tried to lighten the mood. "Can't you just look at porn like the rest of us?"

"Like the rest of you," he said, all dry. "Sure."

"Jack," I said, reaching out to him. "It's okay with me, all right? It totally is. I won't tell anyone, but it's okay with me."

"Yeah," Jack said, getting up. "That's great, Ant, thanks."

"Jack – "

"No, I gotta go." He went to my bedroom door and then he went out of it.

And I didn't see him again all summer, not for two full months until classes started again, and we both had to pretend like nothing had happened.

THE FINAL WEEKEND

"I'm not joking," Charlie says on the Saturday after he lunged at Jack. "I'm going to kill that little ███████."

"For God's sake," I say, "aren't you in enough trouble already?"

"I would have pounded him if Josh hadn't gotten in the way."

"Charlie, we're kind of in the middle of something here."

Charlie didn't get suspended for attacking Jack, which is some kind of miracle, but he'd never been in trouble before, really, even with his loud mouth. Plus, Mr. Bacon is soft, so all that really happened was that Charlie got hauled before the vice principal and given a shellacking and now Charlie has to write a letter of apology to Jack and to Mr. Bacon for disrupting the class. Like writing letters is ever going to fix anything, but there you go, it's better than suspension.

"Are you trying out for soccer on Monday?" Charlie asks.

"Charlie, seriously, are we going to do this or – "

"I said, are you trying out for *soccer on Monday?*"

I lean back away from him. "What do you think?"

He looks at me, and his eyes are like someone I barely even know, like someone *no one* can know. "I think you're trying out for football."

I nearly yell in frustration. "When have I *ever* said that?"

"███ this," he says, reaching over to grab his shirt where he dropped it on the floor. "I don't need this ███ right now. None of it."

"Charlie."

And I grab his shoulder to stop him, his bare shoulder, and for a second there, everything stops. He

looks back at me, and I can feel his skin under my fingertips, I can feel his heartbeat coming down from his neck, I can feel the warmth of him just humming there, and he's looking back at me, all affronted and angry, but still the Charlie I know, still the Charlie I've known for all these years, and also the one I've known for the past ten months since Christmas, the one that only *I* know.

And I do a stupid thing.

I lean forward, my face heading toward Charlie's, and for a second, for a real second there, he doesn't move, he sees me coming and he doesn't move, his eyes full of fear but his head steady, and I'm going to kiss him, going to kiss him right on the mouth –

He shoves me, *hard*. "Get off me!" he says, jumping out of bed and pulling his shirt over his head. He starts kicking our clothes around on the floor, finding his jeans and pulling them on.

"Charlie," I say.

But he's already storming out, still buttoning up his fly, his shoes tucked under his arm, and I hope my mom doesn't see him as he goes or God knows what she'll think.

PARENTS

A little while later, there's a knock on my door. "Yeah?" I say.

"Everything all right, sweetheart?" my mom says, leaning her head in.

"Yeah," I say. "Charlie just got in trouble at school is all. He'll calm down. He always does."

Mom looks sad for a minute. She's known Charlie as long as I have. Known his mom even longer.

"You're a good boy, being such a friend to him," she says.

She nods at me with a smile and closes the door.

Parents. I mean, seriously.

A TEXT

Later, I get a buzz on my phone.

A text from Josh about football.

That's it. Just football.

But I feel a little feeling anyway. And then some other stuff that would really need a black box.

THE DAY THE WORLD ENDS

Monday comes. That's the day it happens.

"Did you bring your gear?" Charlie says, thumping down in the seat next to me in our quad. He's hostile all over the place, but I know he's telling me he's going to forget about what happened on Saturday, that we can just move on and pretend nothing happened.

Like we always do.

"I brought my gear," I say.

"*Soccer* gear?"

I sigh, because, yeah, despite the message I sent back to Josh (about football, that's all), this morning when I packed my bag, it wasn't with football stuff. "Yeah, soccer gear, but Charlie – "

"We'll make varsity this year," he says, almost making it sound like a threat. "You just watch. Un-███████-stoppable."

"You probably won't make varsity, Ant," Josh says, sitting down, Jack coming in behind him. "You still have to learn the game, but I think you could be varsity next year, no problem."

Charlie just stares at him for a second, figuring out what he means. Then he stares at *me*.

"Yeah, Josh, look," I say, feeling Charlie's eyes on me. "I changed my mind. I'm going to try out for soccer with Charlie again."

"*Changed your mind?*" Charlie says. "When had you ever made it up in the first place?"

"Charlie – "

"You said soccer. You *swore* it would be soccer."

"Josh asked me to think about it," I say, "so I thought about it. That's all."

"We've always played soccer," Charlie says.

"And we're going to play it this year. What are you so mad about?"

"You'd be perfect for football, Ant," Jack says, ███-stirring.

"Shut the ███ up!" Charlie says, too loud.

"Mr. Shepton!" Mr. Bacon calls from the front. "You're

already on thin ice. One more word and I'm sending you back to the vice principal."

"You sure about this, Ant?" Josh asks, lowering his voice.

I look at Charlie, still fuming. "Yeah," I say. "I'm sure."

Josh frowns at me. "Whatever, dude."

My stomach hurts at the way he says it. And the hurt must be on my face, too, because Jack sees it.

And that's when it happens. A few little words are all it takes.

"Watch out, Charlie," Jack says, smirking. "You've got competition for the wife."

And Charlie's eyes go wide, too wide, for a second too long, and though he's immediately pulling back and just being angry Charlie again, I see Jack look confused. And then surprised. *Really* surprised.

"*Jack,*" I say, warning in my voice before I can stop myself.

Because I'm sure, I'm *absolutely* sure Jack wouldn't be teasing this way if he thought it was true.

And I know this because I see him realize it the second

I warn him like that.

"No way," Jack says, under his breath.

"No way *what?*" Josh says.

"Hey, ▮▮ you!" Charlie practically shouts at Jack.

"That's it, Charlie!" Mr. Bacon says, approaching our stupid little quad. "Out!"

"Charlie – " I say.

"No way what?" Josh says again.

And I see Charlie's fists clenching and he's getting all red as he's staring at the wondering face of Jack, who's now looking over at me all astonished, and Josh is looking at us like what the hell's going on, and the whole class is looking, too, and it suddenly feels like I'm naked there and everyone can see and everyone knows.

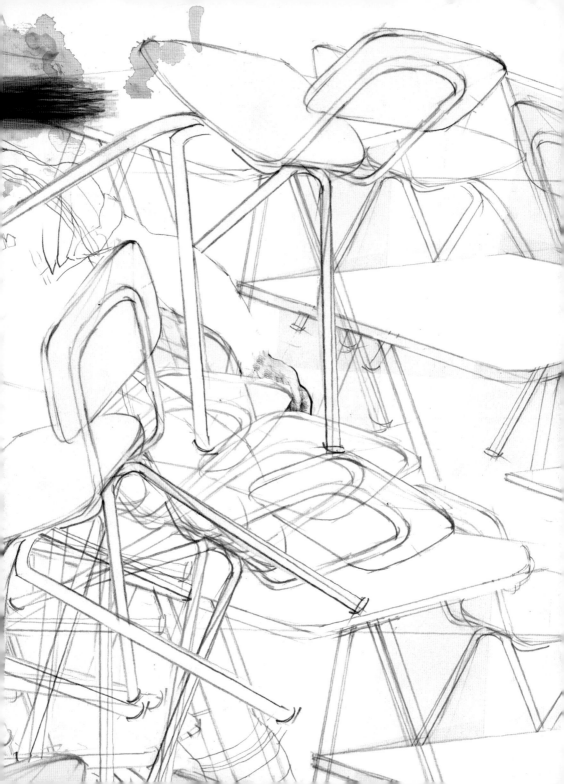

I see the confusion on Charlie's face, the *pain* on it, and Mr. Bacon is approaching fast and Charlie's fists are up and here are all the people in the world he wants to hit, to take out all his Charlie pain on: Jack, who he's made into his worst enemy; Josh, who tried to make me play football; and even Mr. Bacon, who's in the wrong place at the wrong time.

But it's not any of them that he hits.

It's me.

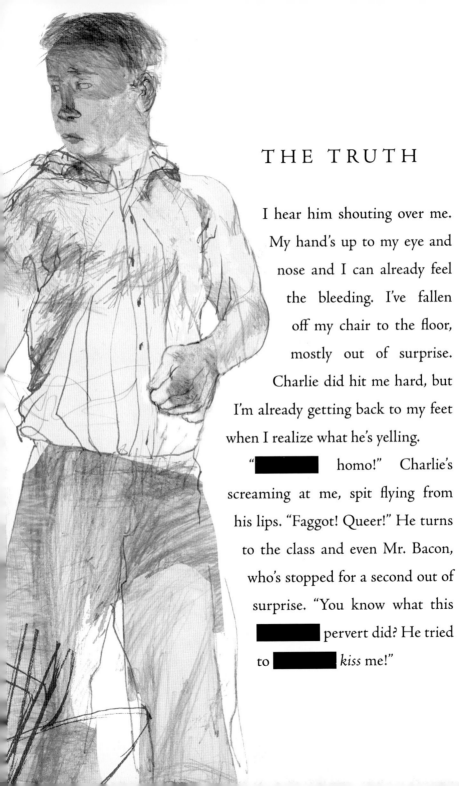

THE TRUTH

I hear him shouting over me.
My hand's up to my eye and
nose and I can already feel
the bleeding. I've fallen
off my chair to the floor,
mostly out of surprise.
Charlie did hit me hard, but
I'm already getting back to my feet
when I realize what he's yelling.

"███████ homo!" Charlie's
screaming at me, spit flying from
his lips. "Faggot! Queer!" He turns
to the class and even Mr. Bacon,
who's stopped for a second out of
surprise. "You know what this
███████ pervert did? He tried
to ███████ *kiss* me!"

And I hear snorts of surprise from the class and I see the faces already starting to laugh.

Not Josh or Jack, though, who are just staring at me.

"He tried to put his ▮▮▮▮▮ hands all *over* me!" Charlie's still screaming. "Ant Stevenson is a ▮▮▮▮▮ faggot!"

"Enough!" Mr. Bacon yells, finally getting moving.

"Deny it!" Charlie's screaming, pointing at my face. "Go on, deny it!"

I'm standing up again, taller than even Mr. Bacon and way bigger than Charlie, but I'm speechless. I'm just looking at Jack and Josh, watching them see me not deny it, watching them realize it might be true, that it *is* true.

Why aren't I shouting back? Why can't I yell back all the things that Charlie and I have done together? That he's ▮▮▮▮▮▮▮▮▮▮ me. That I've ▮▮▮▮▮▮▮▮▮▮ him. That he's done all these things, willingly, *enthusiastically*.

With a word, I could bring him down, bring him down as bad as he's bringing me down now.

But I'm not.

Because it's Charlie.

Even now, I can see how scared he is. How he believed all along that I wouldn't stay with him, that I'd pick Josh over him the second Josh walked in the door, that it's not even a sex thing with Charlie.

It's that he doesn't believe anyone would ever bother being his friend. That he's as lonely as I am.

And that it was only a matter of time before I abandoned him to it.

"Come with me *now*, Charlie," Mr. Bacon says, pulling him away and looking at me. "Get to the nurse, Ant."

Charlie's not yelling anymore, and he gives me a last angry look as Mr. Bacon takes him out of class.

The rest of the class just stare at me, whispering between themselves. Laughing.

Jack and Josh are still watching me. And I know they know it's true. Even if I did deny it now, it'd be too late. Plus it makes sense once someone points it out, doesn't it?

"You ought to get to the nurse," Josh finally says. "That's bleeding pretty bad."

I wait for a second before I go.

Because somehow that feels like the last friendly thing anyone's ever going to say to me.

THE AFTERLIFE

The rest of the day is terrible. I won't lie. I go to the nurse, and by the time she's finished, it's all over.

Charlie got completely kicked out of school. Not just for punching me in the face, but for "homophobic bullying," too, a verdict that passes around the school even faster than what Charlie said and pretty much seals my fate.

People stare at me as I walk by, and there's like this force field around me on all sides that no one would dare to cross. I don't know why I don't lie about it, why I don't counterargue, why I don't make Charlie the one in the force field.

Well, yes, I do, I guess.

I didn't think it was possible to feel lonelier. But there you go. Life will always surprise you with what it's capable of, eh?

There are only two more classes left in the day, neither one with Jack or Josh, classes that I usually had with

Charlie, so not only do I have everyone staring at me, there's an empty desk next to me to give them more room to do it.

I make it through. I don't know how. And as I leave the school grounds with the force field still in place and a group of boys singing "Homo, homo," just loud enough for me to hear it, I don't know how I'm going to make it through a whole school year of this.

And then.

AND THEN

"Hey, Ant," I hear a voice call. "Wait up!"

I turn to see Josh jogging up after me. I stop, but I've never been so aware of eyes on me. On us.

"Hey," he says. "How's the face?"

"It doesn't hurt," I lie.

He just nods, then he looks at the ground. Again, I can feel all the eyes on us, and I can't believe Josh is risking so much guilt by association.

He glances back up at me. "I'm guessing there's some stuff here I don't know."

I don't say anything, just look away.

"But I'm thinking this probably means you can try out for football now?" he says.

I look up. "What?"

He shrugs. "If you can take a hit like that and get right back up, that's pretty much all football is. You're made for it."

"Josh – "

"You're going to get ▮▮▮," he interrupts, looking around at the staring eyes on us, holding them until they look away. "Everyone's going to give you ▮▮ for a while." He shrugs again. "So what you got to do is make sure they know you don't care. Show them you don't. Try out for football. It'll pass."

"You don't . . ." I swallow, still tasting the blood at the back of my throat. "You don't care?"

He grins. "As long as you don't try to kiss *me*."

I stare at him, unbelieving.

"Look, I'm late for tryouts," he says. "But the next one's on Wednesday." He hits me hard on the shoulder. "I expect to see you there, bruiser."

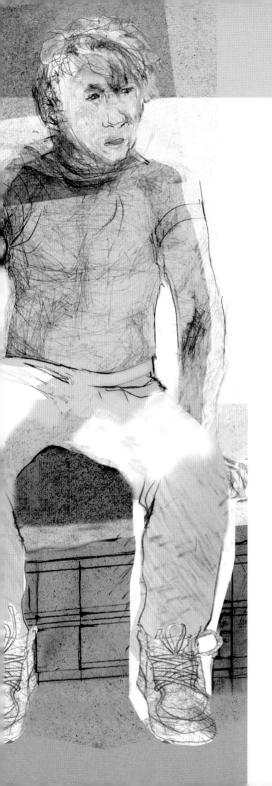

THE EVENING AFTER THE END OF THE WORLD

The doorbell rings about six that evening. I hear it from my room, where I'm busy spending my time avoiding doing Mr. Bacon's history homework. A minute later, there's a knock on my bedroom door. I think it's my mom, so I just say, "What?"

But it's Jack who pokes his head in.

I don't say anything when I see him, so he just steps in the room and shuts the door. We stare at each other for a second.

"Your mom thinks you did that playing football," he finally says, nodding at my black eye.

"Parents say they want to know the truth," I say, "but they never really mean it."

"Tell me about it," he says, crossing his arms, looking at the floor, the walls, anything but my face.

"If you came here for an apology," I say, "I'm sorry."

He glances at me. "Apology for what?"

"Over the summer," I say. "You tried to tell me and I – "

"Oh please," he says. "Like I didn't know you were lying."

I blink. "You knew?"

"It was obvious," he says. "Well, obvious to *me*, but that's probably only because I was looking." He makes a surprised face. "Didn't know about you and Charlie, though. That was a shocker." He laughs once, then looks more serious. "If I'd known, I wouldn't have teased you."

"I know," I say.

He's quiet for a minute and then finally comes away from the door, flopping down on the edge of my bed, next to me but not too close. "It isn't easy," he says, "having people think that about you. But most of them don't care, not *really*. They just love having something new to beat you up with. You have to show them it won't work, and then they'll go back to killing Redheaded Mike."

I breathe out, long and tired. "That's what Josh said."

"Ah, big lovely Josh." Jack looks over at me. "Straight, you know. No matter how much you wish he wasn't."

"I know," I say. "I have to say, as stupid as it sounds, I don't think Charlie's gay either. I think he just needed someone. Someone who cared only for him."

Jack sighs. "You always *were* softhearted, Ant."

"Thanks."

"No, I meant soft*headed*."

"That, too."

And for a minute, it feels like I'm going to cry, it really does, about how empty it all feels, about how difficult things are going to be at school for a while, about how much relief there is to still having friends like Josh and Jack.

About how mad I am at Charlie.

About how bad it feels, too, that I've lost him.

I don't think Jack knows what to do with me looking so upset, so he starts awkwardly slapping me on the back, like he's trying to comfort me but is a little afraid to.

"It'll be all right," he says. "It will, you know. School will be fine, and even if it isn't, school isn't the rest of your life. Not even close."

"I know," I say, my voice a little rough.

We just sit there like that for a long, long time, letting night fall outside, not saying anything at all, just the two of us sitting there, waiting for the month or year or whenever in our lives where we're allowed to stop being lonely.

"Jack," I say, when it's almost too dark to see. "Can I ask you something? Something I've always wanted to know?"

"Okay," he says, a little suspiciously.

I turn to him. "Mark Ruffalo? Over all the others?"

Jack seems surprised into an honest answer. "He looks like he'd never hurt you."

I don't know what to say to this, so I don't say anything, just lower my eyes.

"Plus," Jack says, "he walks like he's making milkshakes in his pockets."

I snort with laughter.

"What?" Jack says, all innocent-sounding. "I like *cooking*."

I laugh again. And then I look at him to find he's looking back at me.

"Can I make a guess about something?" he says.

"What?" I ask.

And he leans forward, just a little, then a little more.

And I don't move toward him. But I don't move back either.

And he reaches me.

And he kisses me.

Gently, so as not to bump my nose or eye, he presses his lips to mine.

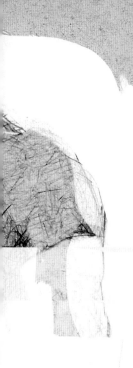

And for a second, for a minute, forever, every nerve in my body is right there, *right* at the point where we're touching.

And *boom*, I think.

That's it.

DIFFERENT FOR BOYS

I do think it's different for boys, boys like me anyway. I think I get to choose when I stop calling myself a virgin. I don't think there are any rules or any specific moment where anyone can say, yep, that's it, that's where you're not a virgin anymore.

I think *I'm* the one who says.

Because nothing I did with Charlie ever once felt like that kiss with Jack.

And yeah, it'd be romantic and swooning and a perfect ending for the story if that kiss was all we ended up doing.

But please, we're teenage boys with teenage hormones and no chance of anyone getting pregnant. What do you *think* we did next? I'll tell you. We ██████████████████████████████████ and then we ████████████████████████████████████ ██████████████████████████████, which was unbelievably great so we ████████████████████████████████

████████████████████████ and then we ████

███████████████████████████████

████████████████ and then we ██████████

███████████████████████████████

██████████████.

And then, after a while, it all sort of morphed into us just talking, which we did for a bit and then a bit more than that and then Jack went home.

Now don't get me wrong here, I'm not saying this is the moment where I found the love of my life. Jack's a really nice guy and a good friend but I'm not really his type – I look *nothing* like Mark Ruffalo – and he's probably not really mine, come to think of it. Besides, there's a whole life out there left for both of us.

At least, now it feels like there might be one.

And I won't say for sure if it was the kiss that felt like the moment when I lost my virginity, #6 added to the list, because now that I think about it, that really is the kind of private thing that should go behind a black box and not all of this swearing and sex crap. You can only lose it

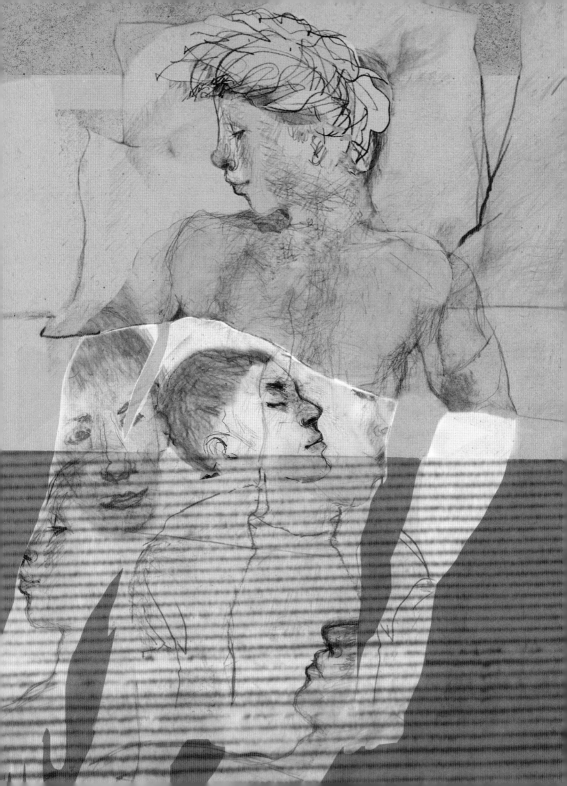

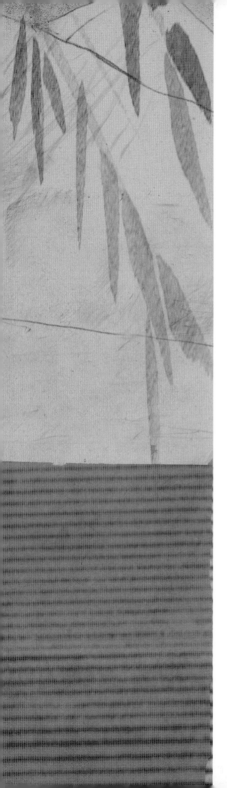

once, and maybe, finally, it's just private.

████████████████████████,
you know?

But I will say this.

Through that whole night, all of it, I didn't sleep a wink. I was worried about the next day at school, sure I was, but I also kept putting my hand up to my lips, pressing them lightly, feeling where Jack's lips touched mine, actually *touched* them.

Just to keep reminding myself that it actually happened.